Isabelle Harper

MY CATS
NICK & NORA

Illustrated by Barry Moser

SCHOLASTIC INC.

New York   Toronto   London   Auckland   Sydney

Izzy, Emmie, and Barry wish to thank Friskies Pet Care, a division of
Nestlé/Carnation Food Company, as well as MILK-BONE, a division of
Nabisco, Inc., for permission to use their pet food in this book.
Friskies is a registered trademark of Nestlé Inc. MILK-BONE® is a
registered trademark of Nabisco, Inc.

ISBN 0-590-47635-1

12 11 10 9 8 7 6 5 4 3 2   12   6 7 8 9/9 0 1/0

Printed in the U.S.A.   08

The illustrations in this book were executed with watercolor on paper handmade by
Simon Green at the Barcham Green Mills in Maidstone, Kent, Great Britain, especially for the
Royal Watercolor Society.

For Sam, Mehitabel, Rufus, Tweed, Big Momma, Smokey, Calhoun, Jenny-Any-Dots, Minnie-One-Dot, Curtis, Dusty & Toasty, Yard Boss, and all the other wonderful cats who have graced our lives

EVERY SUNDAY when my cousin Emmie comes over
to my house, the first thing we do is go find Nick and Nora.

It isn't always easy.
They have lots of places to hide.

But no matter where they hide,
we always find them.

We give them their lessons . . .

We invite all their friends . . .

. . . and have a birthday party.

After the party, we take Nick and Nora for a walk.

Our neighbor Fluffy sees us.

He wasn't invited to the party because he's not nice.

He likes to fight.

And sometimes Nick and Nora are not nice,
either, no matter how pretty they look.

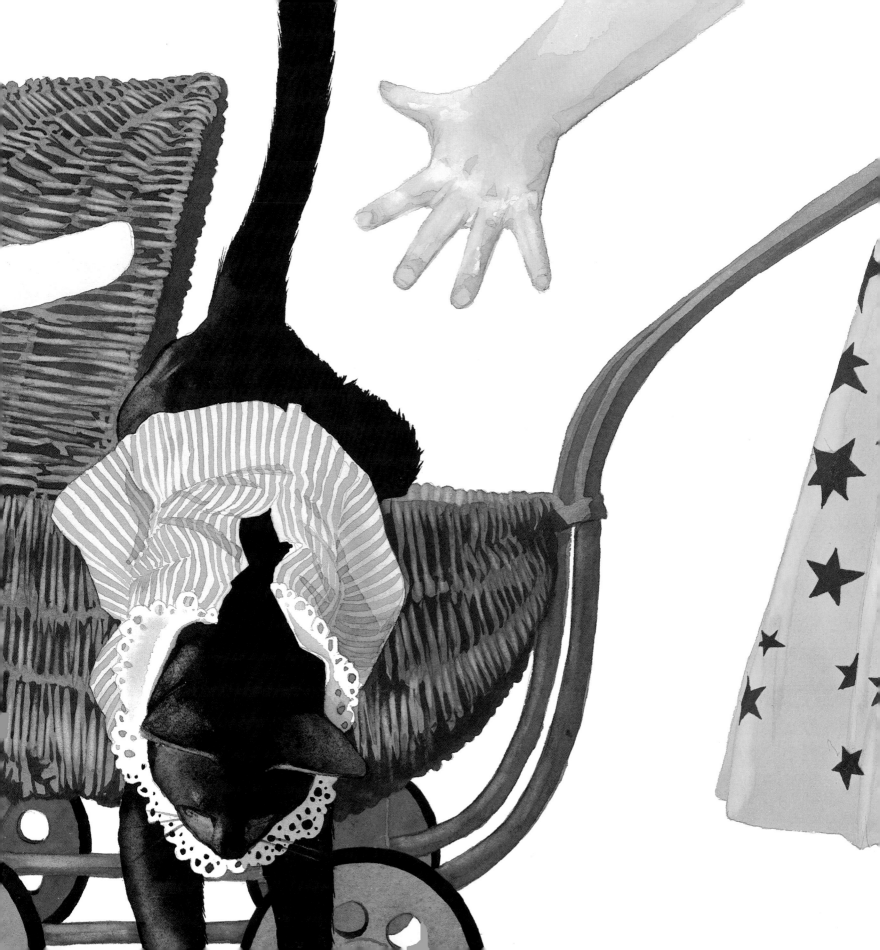

This isn't the first time Fluffy has ruined
our Sunday afternoon walk.

Emmie and I go back to my house.
We don't see Nick or Nora anywhere.

But we're not worried. We know exactly
what will bring them home.

And when Nick and Nora do
come back, we can see they are
tired and ready for their nap.

And so are we.